Contents

Do you like the dark?

✸ Have you been out in the dark?
What was it like?
What did you see?

✸ Which animals like the dark?
What do they do in the dark?

Some people are afraid of the dark.

✸ Tell them why the dark is not frightening.

2

In the dark

Write your ideas on Task Sheet 1.

Sources of light

Many things give light.

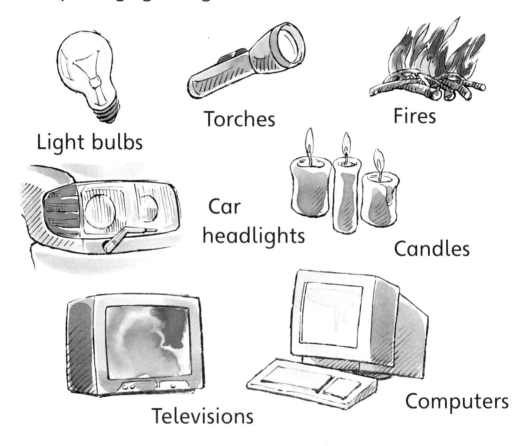

Light bulbs

Torches

Fires

Car
headlights

Candles

Televisions

Computers

The biggest, brightest light source
of all is the Sun.

✿ Name the light sources on Task Sheet 2.

Which is the brighter light?

Alan has a torch.
His friend Luther has a bike lamp.

They want to know which is brighter.

❂ Which light source is brighter?

❂ Think of some ways you could find out.

4 Comparing light sources

⚡ Use two light sources.
Find out which is stronger.
Write your answers on Task Sheet 3.

Castle dungeons

Many old castles had dark dungeons. People needed a light source to help them see in the dungeons.

You cannot see without a light source.

✵ When have you been in the dark?

✵ What could you see?

✵ Complete Task Sheet 4.

Task
6 Make a black box

1 Cut a small hole in the side of a box.
2 Put something in the box.
3 Close the lid.
4 Ask a friend to peep through the hole.
5 What can they see?

YOU NEED:

scissors

empty shoe box

✴ Open the lid a little. What can they see now?

✴ Now take the lid off. What can they see now?

✴ Why could they not see things when the lid was on?

✴ Fill in Task Sheet 5.

The cloudy day

Anne and Caroline went into the playground.

"I'm cold," said Anne.

"It's a very cloudy day," said Caroline.

Then, the Sun came out.

The girls knew they mustn't look at the Sun.

✵ How did the girls know the Sun was out?

✵ Finish this sentence in different ways:
The girls knew the Sun was out because....

9

8 Sunset

The Sun sets at the end of every day.
The sky may be full of different colours.

It gets dark.
Stars appear.
People switch lights on.

It stays dark until the next morning.

YOU NEED:

paints

paint brush

black, yellow and white paper

✳ Paint a sunset. Use lots of colours.
Show dark buildings with the lights on.

1 Paint colours across the page. Let it dry.

2 Cut out and stick or paint black buildings. Stick yellow windows on the buildings.

Wear something shiny at night

Amil has been for a bike ride with his Dad.
Now it is getting dark.

"Switch your lights on," says his Dad.
Amil switches the bike lights on.
He follows his Dad.

He sees his lights reflected.

- Light is reflected
  from his Dad's bike.

- Light is reflected
  from his Dad's pedals.

- Light is reflected
  from his Dad's belt.

✨ How do reflectors help
keep bike riders safe?

✨ Complete Task Sheet 6.

10 Test your reflectors

✴ Use some things that reflect light.
Test them somewhere dark.
Test them in a safe, bright light.

✴ How well do they reflect?

✴ Copy and complete this sentence:
My reflectors worked because ...

✴ Which reflector would help keep you safe
at night? How?

11 Safe in the dark

Zoe has a pony called Dawn.
She rides Dawn on the road.
She rides Dawn after school.

Some days it is starting to get dark when Zoe gets home.

✺ Tell Zoe how she and Dawn can be safe in the dark.

✺ How can Zoe make herself easy to see?
What will car drivers see easily?

✺ Complete Task Sheet 7.

Bonfire Night

In the park,
In the dark,
Rockets

Sparkle

Whizzers

Whizz

Fountains

Dazzle

Fizzers

Fizz

In the park,
In the dark,
The sky's alight
On Bonfire Night!

✪ What sources of light can you see on Bonfire Night?